Alice in America-Land

*or Through the Picture Tube and
What Alice Found There*

by Dennis Snee

Baker's Plays
7611 Sunset Blvd.
Los Angeles, CA 90042
bakersplays.com

CAST OF CHARACTERS

(In Order of Appearance)

ALICE
ANNOUNCER
WHITE RABBIT
MOCK TURTLE
CATERPILLAR
MOUSE
DODO
EAGLE
DUKE
DUCHESS
CHESHIRE CAT
HARE
HATTER
KING

QUEEN
P.R. MAN
STENOGRAPHER
ARAB
RED QUEEN
GENTLEMAN DRESSED
  IN WHITE PAPER
TWEEDLEDUM
TWEEDLEDEE
WHITE QUEEN
HUMPTY DUMPTY
WHITE KNIGHT
PITCHWOMAN
TWO WOMEN
PITCHMAN

ALICE IN AMERICA-LAND

ACT ONE

TIME: *The present.*

SETTING: *The living room/family den at ALICE's home. In an area D.L. are a stuffed chair and a large console-type TV set. TV is turned to face away from audience. A background flat of a bookcase or window and drapes can be used.*

AT RISE: *ALICE, a young girl, is pouring some cat food from a box into a dish. After this, she begins trying to entice her cat, Dinah, to come from offstage, L., to eat its dinner.*

ALICE. Dinah—it's dinner time. Dinah? It's your favorite. Acme cat food. (*No response from Dinah*) New, improved Acme cat food. (*Stern*) Dinah! (*Nothing. She reads from box*) "New, improved Acme cat food . . delicious tuna and chicken—fortified with vitamins and minerals . . . it's the one cat food kitty can't resist . . ." (*Stern again*) Dinah! (*Giving up for the moment, she crosses to TV and puts the dish and box on top of it. She turns on the TV and over the P.A. system we hear an announcer's voice*)

ANNOUNCER. (*Off stage*) . . . remember, that's new,

improved Acme cat food—the cat food no kitty can resist...

ALICE. That's not true!

ANNOUNCER. (*Off stage*) New, improved Acme— the perfect cat food...

ALICE. And you're a perfect liar!

ANNOUNCER. (*Off stage*) Careful, little girl...

ALICE. You should be ashamed of yourself! Telling people things that aren't so.

ANNOUNCER. (*Off stage*) Acme cat food is a division of General Products Corporation—and with assets over 14 billion dollars—we can tell people anything we like.

ALICE. And what if everyone did that?

ANNOUNCER. (*Off stage*) Don't they?

ALICE. Really, you are very despicable. I think if I could see you face to face—

ANNOUNCER. (*Off stage*) And why don't you?

ALICE. (*Puzzled*) Why ... Because ...

ANNOUNCER. (*Off stage*) Don't be bashful. Step right in.

ALICE. What .. ?

ANNOUNCER. (*Off stage*) Step right in ... (*She moves close enough and discovers she can put one leg into the set, through opening where picture tube would otherwise be*)

ALICE. Why...I can...! (*Lights start down as ALICE is climbing in*)

ANNOUNCER. (*Off stage*) Of course you can. With new Acme cat food, (*Lights completely down now*) anything is possible. From General Products Corporation—and remember our motto—"Helping products, to help people, to help us." Or, in the words of our founder:

"Twas brillig, and the slithy toves
did gyre and gimble in the wabe;
all mimsy were the borogoves,
and the mome raths outgrabe.

Beware the jabberwock, my son!
The jaws that bite, the claws that catch!
Beware the Jubjub bird, and shun
The frumious Bandersnatch!"

But time is up and so we too
Will end our discourse and confess;
Your actual grasp within this zoo
Will probably be less . . .

(Lights up full on ALICE U.C. in front of a flat. In the middle of the flat is a small door, about 18" high. Otherwise stage is bare. ALICE looks around, wondering, among other things, where the voice went to)

ALICE. What a strange motto. . . *(Looking around)* What a strange place. . . *(A little unsure now, but with false bravado)* Well, I think I'll just go back through the screen now. If I . . . can find out where it is . . . *(Looking around, she finally notices the door, and crosses to it. She kneels down and eagerly looks through the small panel of glass—or celophane)* Oh . . ! What a beautiful, beautiful garden! Gee, I'd like to go in . . . such bright flowers . . and a swimming pool . . and a jacuzzi! *(She tries the knob on the door; it's locked. Disappointed, she looks around. At D.L., a small stool or table has been either lowered, or pulled onstage with black wire or string. ALICE sees the table, and crosses to it)* I didn't notice this before... *(On the table are a small bottle and a skeleton key)* A key! *(She takes it and returns quickly to the door. As she fiddles with the key in the lock, the WHITE RABBIT enters, right, looking around, and especially above, with a nervous expression)*

WHITE RABBIT. The big one...The big one... What if...What if...

ALICE. *(Seeing the WHITE RABBIT)* Excuse me—

WHITE RABBIT. What is it?

ALICE. I'd like to get into that garden, but this key doesn't seem to work.

WHITE RABBIT. *(Pointing to door)* In there?

ALICE. Yes.

WHITE RABBIT. Can't do it. They're full up. *(Looking up again)* Oh boy...Oh boy... *(Crossing to the exit, left)* The big one...

ALICE. *(She watches him leave, then)* I've never seen a rabbit like that before. *(Considers it, then turns her attention to the door)* Even if I could open that door, how could I fit through? It's much too small. Or—I'm much too big. *(Crossing to put key back on table)* Either it has to get bigger, or I have to get smaller. *(Puts key down, picks up bottle. She reads the label aloud)* "New, improved 'Drink 'N Shrink..'...By Acme, a division of General Products Corporation." *(Puts bottle down)* I certainly won't drink that. It would probably make me twice as *large*, and then what would I do? *(She turns away, resolved. But after a few moments, she wavers)* Of course, I don't have much to lose. *(Regarding door again)* If I did become twice as large, maybe I could jump over this wall, and get into the garden that way...It is such a beautiful place... *(Goes

to the table) I suppose as long as it's not poison...
(*Picks up the bottle again. Reads aloud from label*)
"Definitely not poison." (*She opens the cap and
sniffs the contents*) Smells alright. (*She stands, then
looks at the door, then at the bottle, then takes
a drink. She closes her eyes as she swallows. She
opens them expectantly, but quickly sees she hasn't
changed size. Puts the bottle down*) I should have
known! (*MOCK TURTLE enters, left, on the tail of
this*) Drink and shrink indeed! Those people should
be investigated by the...by the...

MOCK TURTLE. Consumer protection agency.

ALICE. (*Turning*) Who are you?

MOCK TURTLE. I'm a friend of the consumer. And
a corporate critic. (*Crossing to table*) And right now
I intend to get to the bottom of this. I'll go right
to the top! Unfortunately, at present, I'm stuck in
the middle. (*Picks up bottle and looks at it*) "Drink
and Shrink." (*To Alice*) They should call it "Buy
and Cry." (*Puts it down*) Do you have "proof of
purchase?"

ALICE. For what?

MOCK TURTLE. For this.

ALICE. I didn't buy it.

MOCK TURTLE. I see. You're a shoplifter.

ALICE. Certainly not.

MOCK TURTLE. Shoplifting increases—by one and
a half percent—the cost of every item sold. Over
the counter or under the counter. Now there's food
for thought.

ALICE. You don't understand. I was looking through
that door, and when I turned around, I found that
there. (*Bottle and table*)

MOCK TURTLE. Found it?

ALICE. Yes.

MOCK TURTLE. Well, if you found it, someone must've lost it. Lost and found—that's the department you want.

ALICE. Oh, I doubt that anyone is looking for this. It's from the General Products Corporation and I'm sure they have more important things to do.

MOCK TURTLE. Really? Like what?

ALICE. Well . . .

MOCK TURTLE. LIKE RIPPING OFF CONSUMERS. (*Very loud, although he doesn't seem to be trying to shout*)

ALICE. (*After jumping back*) You don't have to scream.

MOCK TURTLE. DID I SCREAM? (*ALICE covers her ears; he adjusts something in his ear, then*) I said, "did I scream?"

ALICE. You certainly did.

MOCK TURTLE. Do you know why I screamed? Because of this (*Points to his ear*) hearing aid—whick was manufactured by the medical division of General Products Corporation. When it goes on the blink, I can't tell whether I'm screaming or talking in a whisper. (*He mouths the last few words, his voice dropping off so Alice can't hear the end of the sentence*)

ALICE. I'm sorry?

MOCK TURTLE. Don't be sorry—be angry! Harness your rage; vent your spleen!

ALICE. I meant I didn't understand what you said before.

MOCK TURTLE. (*Sympathetically*) Oh—hard of hearing are you? And at such an early age. (*Takes something from one of his ears*) Here—please (*Offers it to Alice*) you need this more than I do.

ALICE. No thank you.

MOCK TURTLE. You're right. It's a piece of junk.

(*Tosses it over his shoulder to offstage*) My advice to you is—don't buy *anything*. What do manufacturers care about you? All they care about is profits. And stockholders. You're not a stockholder, are you?

ALICE. Oh, no.

MOCK TURTLE. You could become one, you know. You look as if you'd make a very fine stockholder.

ALICE. I'm not sure what a stockholder is.

MOCK TURTLE. I haven't the faintest idea myself—although I do know they're frequently involved in killings.

ALICE. Killings!?

MOCK TURTLE. Then when they make a killing, they brag about it!

ALICE. How awful!

MOCK TURTLE. Of course it's awful. And I'll tell you what's worse.

ALICE. What?

MOCK TURTLE. Toasters.

ALICE. Toasters?

MOCK TURTLE. Or haven't you heard of planned obsolescence?

ALICE. I'm afraid I haven't. (*An idea*) Say—could you help me get in the garden?

MOCK TURTLE. The garden, eh? You don't want to go in there.

ALICE. Oh, but I do!

MOCK TURTLE. Believe me, through that door pass very small people.

ALICE. That's my problem. I'm too big.

MOCK TURTLE. For what? Your britches? You're not even wearing britches. Don't tell me—you bought a pair of expensive designer jeans and the first time you washed them they fell apart. Didn't they?!

ALICE. No.

MOCK TURTLE. No?

ALICE. No.

MOCK TURTLE. (*Extending his hand*) May I shake your hand? You are the first satisfied customer I've met in a long time. (*They shake hands*)

ALICE. Except I'm not very satisfied right now.

MOCK TURTLE. With good reason! Just keep in mind three things. (*Moves to table*) First, it's a jungle out there. Second, (*Picks up bottle*) this stuff is worthless. And third, you have got to knock off the shoplifting. (*ALICE turns away, exasperated*) Something wrong? (*No reply*) You can tell me...(*ALICE breathes a deep sigh of disappointment. TURTLE throws up his hands in resignation, takes ALICE by the wrist and leads her to a spot, D.R. In his other hand he carries the bottle*)...I knew it would come to this. (*They stop. All lights down except spot on them. TURTLE clears his throat, and, announcer-like, announces the song he's about to sing*) A medley—consisting of one song—my very own "Turtle Soup." (*He clears his throat again. During song, back flat with door in it is struck; "garden" background is set—flat with trees, flowers, and all of it very large—twice as big as Alice; he sings his made-up song*)

> Beautiful soup so rich and green,
> Waiting in a hot tureen!
> Who for such dainties would not stoop?
> Soup of the evening, beautiful soup
>
> Soup of the evening, beautiful soup!
> Soup of the evening, beautiful soup
> Beau-ootiful soo-oop!
> Beau-ootiful soo-oop!
> Soo-oop of the e-e-e-evening,
> Beautiful, beautiful soup!

Beautiful soup! Who cares for fish,
Game, or any other dish?
Who would give all else for two-
Pennyworth only of beautiful soup?

Soup of the evening, beautiful soup!
Soup of the evening, beautiful soup!
Beau-ootiful soo-oop!
Beau-ootiful soo-oop!
Soo-oop of the e-e-e-evening,
Beautiful, beautiful soup!

ALICE. (*Applauds*) Thank you—what a lovely song!

MOCK TURTLE. Thank *you* (*He un-caps the bottle*), and I'll drink to that . . .

ALICE. But you said that was worthless.

TURTLE. (*About to drink*) Yeah, but I never hold a grudge. (*He takes a swallow and hands it to ALICE*)

ALICE. Do you think it might make me small enough to get into the garden after all?

TURTLE. Ah . . . No. But then again, I thought Howard Cosell's hair was real. (*ALICE takes a swallow, hands bottle back to TURTLE*) Well, good luck. (*He starts backing off, right*)

ALICE. Wait—where are you going?

MOCK TURTLE. I have to get to a consumer rally.

ALICE. Why?

MOCK TURTLE. To protest the misleading labels on cans of condensed turtle soup. Also, they've asked me to sing the National Anthem. (*Lights start up full*)

ALICE. But. . . (*TURTLE exits with a wave to Alice*) Oh . . . Something's happening . . . I feel like . . . Like . . . (*She moves to U.C. now and the garden background. With full stage lights up, she turns to see the immense foliage garden behind her*) Oh! It worked ... It worked! (*Looking around*) It looks a little different from the inside ...

WHITE RABBIT. (*Entering, he is still looking up, muttering*) The big one ... The big one ... (*But now he is looking on the ground, also*) Where could they be ... Where .. ?

ALICE. (*After watching him*) Pardon me, but didn't I just see you outside the garden?

WHITE RABBIT. No! Say, you haven't seen them, have you?

ALICE. Seen what?

WHITE RABBIT. Seen what? (*Moving closer and looking at her*) It's a good thing you came here when you did. Do you realize we live in the shadow of nuclear annihilation? That there's murder in the air in the best parts of our finest cities? Vandalism, terrorism—aren't you aware of this?

ALICE. .. A little.

WHITE RABBIT. A little? Well, if you're just "a little" aware of these minor concerns, it's no wonder you aren't familiar with the major trauma facing us today.

ALICE. What's a trauma?

WHITE RABBIT. A trauma is a disaster, a catastrophe, in other words—(*Looks around*) I lost the duchess's tickets for the Super Bowl.

ALICE. I see.

WHITE RABBIT. I see too. But I don't see the tickets!! (*He exits, right*)

ALICE. (*Watching him exit*) No. I've never seen a rabbit like that. Not even Bugs Bunny. (*After a moment, she looks around again*) I wonder whose garden this is ... Well, whoever's garden it is, I'm here now and I'm going to have fun ... And I won't pay any attention to how strangely I feel ... To think

that yesterday everything seemed so normal ... Although I did feel different this morning ... Different, yes ... But if I'm not the same, who am I? I could be Mabel ... But then who would she be ... (*Reciting a rhyme*)
"Mabel, Mabel, set the table;
Don't come out until you're able."
(*Looks around*) No. I'm definitely not Mabel ...

CATERPILLAR. (*Entering, right; he smokes a long hookah*) Pst. You are who you are.

ALICE. (*Turning*) Who are you.

CATERPILLAR. I am who I am.

ALICE. You're lucky to know that much. (*Moving toward him*) This is such a strange place, I'd be happy just to know *where* I am.

CATERPILLAR. You are where you are.

ALICE. Really, I wish you wouldn't keep talking like that.

CATERPILLAR. I talk like I talk. Pst. (*Alice turns away, disgusted*) You don't understand.

ALICE. No, I don't.

CATERPILLAR. You are a child of the universe. Unfortunately, this garden is "adults only." Leave.

ALICE. I won't!

CATERPILLAR. (*Taking a long draw on the hookah*) Good.

ALICE. Good? Why do you say good?

CATERPILLAR. You must define your own space and let no one intrude on it.

ALICE. Why?

CATERPILLAR. Unless you don't want to—then you can do whatever you like. Pst.

ALICE. Why do you keep saying "pst?"

CATERPILLAR. "Pst" stands for "personal sensitivity training." That's what I teach.

ALICE. You're a teacher?

CATERPILLAR. Only when I have students.

ALICE. And when you have no students?

CATERPILLAR. When I have no students, I have no students.

ALICE. You wouldn't have me as a student in any event. Talking and making no sense at all. And what kind of teacher would smoke in front of young people?

CATERPILLAR. An apple a day keeps the doctor away.

ALICE. Smoking is quite bad for you. The surgeon general said so.

CATERPILLAR. The sturgeon general selects smoked salmon specifically.

ALICE. It can stunt your growth.

CATERPILLAR. Growth comes from within, not without. Not without pain, not without suffering, not without realization of self.

ALICE. Could you make me grow?

CATERPILLAR. No. But *you* could.

ALICE. If I could grow enough, I'd step out of this garden and away from here.

CATERPILLAR. Accept responsibilty for your own actions.

ALICE. I don't know that I should accept anything from you.

CATERPILLAR. All that you need, you already have.

ALICE. That's perfect nonsense.

CATERPILLAR. Learn to be your own best friend.

ALICE. If the choice were only between myself and you, I wouldn't hesitate.

CATERPILLAR. I'm alright; you're alright.

ALICE. I don't know who said you could call yourself a teacher, but I'm certainly not alright and I have my doubts about you.

CATERPILLAR. (*Assumes a yoga like stance and sound*) Ommm... Ommm...

ALICE. Really you are the strangest caterpillar, even for a place as strange as this.

CATERPILLAR. I am strange because you see me as strange. When you accept yourself in your world, you will be tranquil, and you will control your own destiny.

ALICE. But how can I get to my world? I came through the TV, and now I'm stuck here.

CATERPILLAR. (*Interested*) What kind of TV?

ALICE. (*Thinks, then*) I don't know.

CATERPILLAR. Probably Japanese.

ALICE. Does it matter?

CATERPILLAR. Not to me, but Zenith and Magnavox might be interested.

ALICE. You haven't helped me very much.

CATERPILLAR. I am not here to help you. Pst provides you only with the means of helping yourself. Dig?

ALICE. Fiddlesticks! (*She turns and marches to D.R., stands with arms folded*) This is not the garden I thought it would be. It's perfectly confused and confusing.

WHITE RABBIT. (*Entering, left, still looking up and around nervously*) .. and what about germ warfare .. ? ... maybe a nice little thing in the water supply ...

CATERPILLAR. (*Starting off, left*) Create your own space ...

WHITE RABBIT. (*To Caterpillar*) Why don't you create me a couple of Super Bowl tickets, hey pal?

CATERPILLAR. Become what you are. (*Continuing off; he exits*)

WHITE RABBIT. Hey, I don't know what you're smoking in that .. lamp you have there, but just keep moving. (*Looking up suddenly as if he heard something*) What was that .. !

ALICE. (*Moving toward him*) Pardon me, but—

WHITE RABBIT. (*Turns joyous*) You found them! You found the tickets!!

ALICE. No, I didn't. I—

WHITE RABBIT. (*Crossing immediately, R.*) Oh, the times we live in .. the times we live in ... (*He exits, R.*)

ALICE. (*A little sad*) If I only could be big again ... But the turtle took the bottle ... But the bottle wasn't for becoming big, it was for becoming small ... Oh, I wish Dinah were here ... (*On the tail end of this, the MOUSE, the DODO, and the EAGLE enter, L.*)

MOUSE. Dinah? Who's Dinah?

DODO. (*Who carries a guitar, strums and sings*)
I dream of Dinah,
With the light brown hair ...

EAGLE. Yes—yes, now that's a song! Not like the junk today. Once upon a time there were nickleodeons, and young people respected their elders.

MOUSE. (*As if addressing a crowd in a speech*) We all understand the problems of the elderly. I personally have always advocated that they be treated with dignity and respect. (*To Alice*) But about this Dinah—can she vote? Is she registered?

ALICE. (*Happy to be on a subject dear to her*) Oh, yes, she's quite registered—that is, she has a license. But I don't think she could vote. Cats aren't allowed. And if they could, who would they vote for?

MOUSE. Personally, cats make me a little nervous. However, a vote is a vote, and a vote for yours truly is a vote for myself. Thank you.

ALICE. What are you running for?

MOUSE. (*Proudly*) Cheese!

ALICE. Cheese?

DODO. (*Singing*)
  Three blind mice,
  Three blind mice,
  See how they run.
  See how they run.

  They all ran after the farmer's wife,
  She cut—
MOUSE. (*Cutting the DODO off abruptly*) That's
enough, that's enough, thanks. (*Smiling, to Alice*)
There's nothing like a strolling minstrel, but this
dodo get's carried away. Not that I have anything
against dodos—some of my best friends are dodos—in
fact I intend to introduce some very important dodo
legislation later this week. Thank you very much.
ALICE. (*Crossing for a closer look at the Dodo*)
I've never seen an actual dodo before...
EAGLE. The dodo! Now there was a bird. Couldn't
fly a lick, but they compensated for it by becoming
extinct in the 17th century. Ah, the 17th century...
(*Glowing in the nostalgia of it*) That's when there
was a feeling, a respect for certain values. Space
travel—bah! Give me ships on the sea, locomotives
rumbling down the track. That's what we need!
MOUSE. (*Stepping up and expostulating again*) Nat-
urally, the railroad workers deserve top priority in
any assessment of the current—or future—situations.
ALICE. (*To dodo*) You play very well.
DODO. Thanks. I'll be on tour through the eight-
eenth; Canada, Mexico, then, ah.."Down Under."
MOUSE. Australia?
DODO. No—six feet—down under. My doctor says
this tour's gonna kill me. (*Strums a chord, sings*)
  All my trials, Lord;
  Soon be over...

(*To Alice*) What do you like? Punk? Country-Western? Jazz? Rock 'n Roll? Rock 'n roll's great stuff ... (*He plays a rock chord progression, then, wistfully*) I love rock 'n roll.

EAGLE. Of course you do. Rock 'n roll was made for dodos. (*To Alice*) Glenn Miller. John Philip Sousa. Francis Scott Key! I'm working on a time machine. When it's finished I expect a commission from the queen directing me to return to the fifteenth century to tell Christopher Columbus to forget the whole thing. Deal's off. We'd all be better off in the old world.

MOUSE. (*To Alice*) Speaking of age, a good cheddar should be ripened slowly, which will be my first order of business should the community respond to my particular vision. You wouldn't happen to have, say .. a slice of Swiss on you?

ALICE. (*Feels her pockets*) No ... But would you care for some cat food?

DODO. Would he care for some cat food? He *is* cat food.

MOUSE. There are such things as libel laws, you know.

EAGLE. Take 'em to court!

DODO. Hey—I'll be in Canada ...

MOUSE. (*Walks away, despondent*) It's the story of my life ...

ALICE. What is?

MOUSE. Just when there's a chance to recoup my lost prestige, I remember that the courts would give me no satisfaction.

EAGLE. Balderdash. Take 'em to court.

MOUSE. Mine is a long, sad tale.—(*Holding his tail sadly*)

ALICE. (*Looking at it*) It certainly is long. But why do you say it's sad?

MOUSE. Just listen . . . (*Reading along his tail as if the poem were written on it like a ticker tape*)

"Fury said to a mouse,
that he met in the house,
'Let us both go to law:
I will prosecute *you*—

Come, I'll take no denial,
We must have the trial;
For really this morning
I've nothing to do.'

Said the mouse to the cur,
'Such a trail, dear sir,
With no jury or judge,
Would be wasting our breath.'

'I'll be judge, I'll be jury,'
said cunning old Fury.
'I'll try the whole cause,
and condemn you to death.' "

EAGLE. And there's your criminal justice system for you! Yessir!

MOUSE. (*Brightening*) But, for better or worse, I'm a confirmed optimist. And so, I implore you all to join me now in a caucus race.

ALICE. Oh, good! What kind of race is a caucus race?

MOUSE. Simply put, it's a chance for the electorate and appropriate gentry therein, to make their feelings known, and to form ad hoc committees on a need-to-know basis.

EAGLE. Ready; go!

(*The DODO begins playing his guitar and running
     while the EAGLE runs, stops, runs again in vari-*

circles around the MOUSE, who does a pirouhette, —while the EAGLE runs, stops, runs again in various directions. ALICE joins in, not knowing what to do, but having fun. After a moment the MOUSE yells)

MOUSE. ST-O-O-O-O-P! (*They all do*)

ALICE. (*Laughing*) Oh, could we do it again? Could we?

EAGLE. (*Out of breath*) What do you think this is? The Olympics?

MOUSE. The caucus race is now history. And the winner is . . . (*All lean in to hear*) Everyone!

ALICE. (*Watching DODO, EAGLE and MOUSE shake hands*) But how could *everybody* win?

DODO. Practice, practice, practice.

MOUSE. Yes, all have won, and all must have prizes; emoluments of office, so to speak. (*To Dodo*) You shall become undersecretary to the secretary in charge of junkfood tasting.

DODO. (*Evenly*) I'm overjoyed.

ALICE. You are?

DODO. Can't you see the Twinkie in my eye?

MOUSE. (*To Eagle*) And you—you shall be awarded untold riches, and a home on the lake. Posthumously.

EAGLE. What does "posthumously" mean?

MOUSE. As the new ambassador in charge of explanations, my first order of business will be to find out exactly that. (*To Alice*) Now. What would you like?

ALICE. I'd like to have Dinah here. Right now.

MOUSE. Consider it done.

ALICE. You mean you can do it!?

MOUSE. No, but consider it done, and it'll be just as good.

ALICE. You really shouldn't tease like that.

MOUSE. Nothing could be more true. And in my

secondary position as general consul in charge of apologies, I extend my hand and suggest (*Extending his hand to ALICE; she does the same, but as they're about to shake, he pulls his quickly away*) .. that you "hang it on the wall."

ALICE. That's very rude!

MOUSE. I've decided to take my hat out of the ring. I no longer seek the cheese. And with that, I free myself to speak candidly. Now about this cat, Dinah—YIKES! (*He rushes off, right*)

EAGLE. (*Crosses to left exit, stops and turns*) Anything you'd like me to tell Christopher Columbus?

ALICE. Ah ... I like the names of his ships.

EAGLE. Because they're good names, that's why! Nina, Pinta, Santa Maria—not like today—"Heidi, Heather, Jennifer." All women should be called Jane, and that's that. (*Exits*)

ALICE. (*To DODO*) I suppose you'll be leaving too.

DODO. Gotta get back on the road. But let me show you my latest tape. (*Takes out a roll of scotch tape. Tears off a piece and tapes his lips shut. Waves to Alice, then exits, left, strumming his guitar and trying to sing through his taped lips*)

ALICE. (*Alone again*) I think I might just be better off alone in this place ... Although, it would be nice to have someone to talk to.

WHITE RABBIT. (*Entering on the end of this*) It would be *nice* if I had those tickets.

ALICE. Oh, you again. (*Crossing to him*) You know, maybe you should go to a ticket office.

WHITE RABBIT. Ticket office? Ticket office?? I refuse to go to a ticket office. Let the ticket office come to me.

ALICE. But a ticket office can't do that. Why don't we both go to a ticket office, then maybe you can show me the way home from there.

WHITE RABBIT. (*Shaking his head in disbelief*) We live in constant dread of the big one, and you want to go to some stupid ticket office.

ALICE. For a rabbit, it probably wouldn't take any time at all.

WHITE RABBIT. Sometimes I wish I were a rabbit.

ALICE. But ... You are a rabbit.

WHITE RABBIT. (*Gesturing for her to follow as he moves D.L.*) Come ... Come here where the light is better... (*As they move, all lights come down except for a spot, D.L. In the darkness, garden background is struck. Duke and Duchess' breakfast table is set U.C.*)...come here and witness for yourself a miracle of modern technology... (*They are lighted only by the spot now. RABBIT holds out his arms and turns around slowly, so Alice can get a good look at him*) What you see, is a rabbit. But what I am .. is a rat!

ALICE. Don't say that.

WHITE RABBIT. It's true.

ALICE. It's not nice to call someone a rat. Even yourself. You seem like a very .. nice rabbit. Even if you are confused.

WHITE RABBIT. (*Puts his arms down and looks at her*) My dear, allow me to briefly outline my history. I was born in Montreal; the youngest of seventeen. I was also the smallest rat of the litter. I was recruited by a research laboratory which promised me—(*Thinks*) me? Us! They promised all of us laboratory rats great things. There was talk of a seaside location with plenty of sunshine and healthy salt air. They mentioned lifetime medical insurance. They even talked of retirement benefits. Can you believe it? The audacity of those people, to talk of retirement benefits when it was the probing and prodding and injections and viruses they exposed me to that turned me into the dead ringer for a white rabbit that I am today. Yes, I am a rat. And I have the medical research community to thank for altering my appearance, changing me into the biological halfbreed you see before you now. (*Sighs*) An unfortunate story. (*Brighter*) But, maybe someday, somebody'll turn it into a sitcom.

ALICE. (*Mesmerized by the story*) Gee. What did your parents think of all this?

WHITE RABBIT. Fortunately, I was a test-tube rat.

ALICE. What a story . . . Why don't you tell it to the newspapers?

WHITE RABBIT. The newspapers! (*With disdain*) You know what I—and the rest of the rats—do to newspapers??

ALICE. What?

WHITE RABBIT. Newspapers, television—they're all alike. They only care about us if we're a pioneer of some kind—preferable a gory, disgusting pioneer.

ALICE. I bet if you went to the newspapers and told them that you were a rat, who looked like a rabbit, and needed some tickets for the Super Bowl— (*She stops. It suddenly sounds too implausible even for her*)

WHITE RABBIT. Yes .. ?

ALICE. Maybe it's not such a good idea after all ...

WHITE RABBIT. Look, kid—you've gotta help me ... (*Takes her by the arms; urgent, and a little confidential*) If I take you to the Duke and Duchesses house, will you kind of nose around and see if they're upset about these tickets? Could ya? Would ya? Huh .. ?

ALICE. (*Considers it, then*) I don't suppose I could be any worse off than I am now ...

WHITE RABBIT. 'Course you couldn't! (*As he leads AL-ICE to U.C., lights come up on DUKE and DUCHESS at breakfast table. DUCHESS wears a man's vested business suit, and is seated, reading the Wall Street Journal. DUKE is in a bathrobe; he is just putting a plate of toast and glass of juice in front of DUCHESS)* ..look—they're just having breakfast. The time is perfect—go ahead ..put your "rabbit ears" on... *(He gives her a shove toward table. ALICE moves directly U.C. of table. She stands, listening, as DUKE and DUCHESS seem to be oblivious to her presence)*

DUCHESS. *(From behind paper)* ..says here municipal bonds are getting to be like crooked lawyers—they're everywhere.

DUKE. I wish you wouldn't read at the breakfast table. None of the other duchesses do that.

DUCHESS. *(Puts paper down)* Sorry, dear. But as a Duke, you should understand. I have to keep up on these interest rates; the dukedom could be in chaos with these things.

DUKE. Yes, yes, yes. Now listen, I have to take little Dukie Junior to the dentist today, then I have some shopping to do, and then I'm meeting a few of the other Dukes for a couple of beers. If you can't be home by six, I'll have to call a babysitter.

DUCHESS. No, no. Don't call a babysitter. *(Looks at Alice)* Why can't she babysit?

DUKE. *(Also looks at Alice)* I don't know. Who is she?

DUCHESS. She's the new maid, isn't she? *(To Alice)* Get us some coffee.

DUKE. By the way, since I'm going to meet the other Dukes for a few cold ones, I have to buy myself a new coat-of-arms tee shirt.

DUCHESS. You've got a whole closet full of those things.

DUKE. Half of them don't fit, and half of them are so faded I'm embarrassed to wear them.

DUCHESS. These things cost money, you know.

DUKE. (*Sing-songy; imitating Duchess*) I know they cost money, and if you don't think I deserve an occasional new tee shirt, just tell me.

DUCHESS. Don't be ridiculous. You know I appreciate all the work you do here—you're the best houseduke in the world—but I have to consider the financial side of all this stuff.

DUKE. Honestly, after a while I get so sick and tired of all this financial talk!

DUCHESS. Hey, if you need a new coat of arms tee shirt, get one. All I know is, you're not the only one who works around here. I'm a working duchess, and I bust my chops to put food on the table.

DUKE. Don't make me laugh. The servants put the food on the table! (*To Alice*) Where's the coffee?

ALICE. (*Startled*) I don't know.

DUCHESS. (*To Duke, pointing to Alice*) Another sharp housekeeper you picked here—you've got a good eye for that, you know?

DUKE. So what do you think? You think because you go off every day and make business decisions that making domestic decisions is something any idiot could do?

DUCHESS. What are you getting so defensive about?

DUKE. Nothing! Nothing at all! (*Turns away from table*)

DUCHESS. (*Throwing her hands up*) I can't win. I can't win with this man! (*Picks up the newspaper*) Now you know why I don't put down the paper! (*Puts it down again*) And if you think it's so easy to be out in the working world—why don't you try it? Go on; you'd get eaten alive out there!

DUKE. You don't know what you're talking about. A duke can do anything a duchess can do—at least in this duchy!

DUCHESS. (*Softening*) Look, I don't mean to be a typical narrow-minded duchess. I realize you could do a job just as well as I could.

DUKE. Maybe better.

DUCHESS. Right, maybe better. But let's deal with the situation at hand. A) I may be working late tonight; B) you're meeting the boys for some beers and you need a new shirt, and C) (*To Alice*) WHERE'S THE COFFEE??

ALICE. (*Backing away*) I . . . I don't know . . .

DUCHESS. And don't stammer!

DUKE. Don't you know she (*Points to Duchess*) has a heart condition?

DUCHESS. Do you know what it means when I get upset??

DUKE. (*DUKE and DUCHESS are both moving toward ALICE as she backs away to D.L.*) What's wrong with you! How could you get her so upset??

DUKE AND DUCHESS. How? How!! HOW!!! (*They stop, as ALICE finally backs into the WHITE RABBIT. They are back to back as DUKE and DUCHESS move back to table and all lights are down except on Alice and Rabbit, D.L.*)

WHITE RABBIT. (*To Alice*) So, how'd it go? What'd you find out? (*Breakfast table is struck; Hare and Hatter's table is set in front of building flat while lights are down*)

ALICE. Well, he—I mean, she—I mean—the one that stays home and takes the children to the dentist—that one seems a little irritable.

WHITE RABBIT. That's the Duke.

ALICE. The Duke. And the other one—

WHITE RABBIT. The Duchess.

ALICE. Yes, the Duchess—the one that goes out to work—that one seems irritable, too.

WHITE RABBIT. Hmmm. (*Thinks*)

ALICE. (*Remembering the bright spot*) But—neither one of them said anything about the tickets.

WHITE RABBIT. What tickets?

ALICE. (*Looks at him in amazement*) You silly rabbit! The tickets for the Super Bowl.

WHITE RABBIT. Oh yeah . . . (*He turns and starts walking away*)

ALICE. (*Stopping him*) Wait a minute!

WHITE RABBIT. I'm sorry, but I refuse to talk to the press.

ALICE. I'm not the press.

WHITE RABBIT. I know. (*Pointing over Alice's shoulder*) But she is. (*ALICE turns. RABBIT exits. CHESHIRE CAT enters carrying reporters' pad*)

CHESHIRE CAT. (*To Alice*) Excuse me, but you were talking to that rabbit, correct?

ALICE. Yes I was.

CHESHIRE CAT. Can I ask you a couple of questions?

ALICE. But who are you?

CHESHIRE CAT. I'm with the *Cheshire Daily Enquirer*—special investigative reporter.

ALICE. Can I ask *you* a couple of questions first?

CHESHIRE CAT. Well . . .

ALICE. I mean fair is fair.

CHESHIRE CAT. Well, OK. But I can't reveal my sources.

ALICE. I don't want to know your sources. I'd like to know which way you think I should walk from here.

CHESHIRE CAT. That depends on where you want to get to. Now, my first question—

ALICE. Please— I haven't finished yet. You see, I don't much care where I get to—

CHESHIRE CAT. Then it doesn't matter which way you walk. Now about that rabbit—

ALICE. What kind of people live around here?

CHESHIRE CAT. (*Pointing*) Over there is a Hatter, and over there is a March Hare. Take your pick; they're both mad.

ALICE. (*Doesn't like the idea*) I wouldn't want to be around people that were mad.

CHESHIRE CAT. (*Taking that down on her pad as a quote*)"...discriminates against the mentally deficient.." (*Finishes writing*) Good—now we're getting somewhere.

ALICE. I wouldn't say that. I don't seem to be going anywhere at all.

CHESHIRE CAT. (*Another quote to write down*) "...sees need for more public transportation..."

ALICE. What are you writing?

CHESHIRE CAT. Not sure—haven't decided on a point of view yet. But don't worry, I'll find one. The rabbit. Isn't it true he represents four-star greed? Hob-nobs with the establishment types—duchesses, senators, gas station owners?

ALICE. You really should talk to him. He has the most unbelievable story.

CHESHIRE CAT. (*Writing it down*)"..rabbit a pathological liar, source says." (*Looks up*) What else? What about the connection with radicals and revolutionaries?

ALICE. I don't know anything about that.

CHESHIRE CAT. (*Writing*) "Cannot deny link, says insider..." (*Looks up*) This is great—a few more questions, we'll be all through.

ALICE. Excuse me, but—

CHESHIRE CAT. What do you know about his background?

ALICE. Well he claims he was originally a rat.

CHESHIRE CAT. (*Writing gleefully*) This is terrific—"..admits to war crimes..." (*Looks at Alice*) Say, how'd you like to be on the six o'clock news?

ALICE. Six o'clock? I was hoping I'd be home by six o'clock.

CHESHIRE CAT. What do you want to go home for? You're right in the middle of a big story here.

ALICE. I am?

CHESHIRE CAT. (*Looks around, confidential*) Listen —if you can provide me with this kind of information on a regular basis—

ALICE. What information?

CHESHIRE CAT. You know, about the rabbit. For today I only need a few more things—but in the future, I mean, you'd be providing the public a great service.

ALICE. I would?

CHESHIRE CAT. The public has a right to know. And you have an obligation to tell.

ALICE. Tell what?

CHESHIRE CAT. Whatever's true, and factual, and can be verified, and is juicy, hard hitting, and sensational! Get it?

ALICE. Ah . . . No.

CHESHIRE CAT. Good. (*Takes ALICE'S arm, leading her U.C.*) What do you say we go to your house and I'll send for a mini-cam; we'll get everything down. That way everything'll be straight from the horses mouth.

ALICE. Well, I certainly would be happy if you could take me home. (*Lights are up full now. HARE and HATTER sit at "banquet" table. Both sit staring into space, apparently bored. A tea set and some sandwiches are on the table—a picnic table would work here*)

CHESHIRE CAT. Hey, now wait a minute, let's back up here. I can't furnish you with any kind of payment for this. That'd be like buying the information. You understand.

ALICE. Not exactly.

CHESHIRE CAT. Tell you what. I've got enough here (*Looking at pad*) for maybe a three-part series. I'll catch up with you for any fill-in stuff I need later, OK? And thanks again! (*Starts off, Right. Calls to offstage*) Stop the presses!! Or at least slow 'em down . . .

ALICE. (*Watching cat exit*) I don't know if I'll ever get home if I have to depend on help from these people . . .

HARE. (*Jumping to his feet as if he's just gotten a cue. Both he and Hatter work as if at a roast*) And *people* are the reason we're *honoring* (*Winks at Hatter*) this very special guest today . . . (*Alice moves to table*)

HATTER. (*Standing*) This young woman—our little lady here—is real people. Just plain folks. And— (*ALICE sits now, watching in fascination*) she is also a person of intelligence, beauty, and charm. And that's not just my opinion—it's her's! (*HARE and HATTER break up laughing. Which they do after every joke*)

HARE. But we're here to compliment Alice, because she certainly knows how to give a compliment herself. She once told me that if I swallowed a fly, I'd have more brains in my stomach than in my head. (*HARE and HATTER roar. ALICE is enjoying it*)

HATTER. And I don't want to say Alice considers herself to be important, but she's the only person I know who calls Dial a Prayer and asks if she has any messages . . .

HARE. Actually, people have said on occasion that Alice is not the smartest girl in the world. That if you gave Alice a zebra, she'd call him "Spot."

HATTER. Today Alice is a beautiful young lady—but as a baby—ohhh, was she ugly!

HARE. How ugly? How ugly was she??

HATTER. You've heard of getting hit with the ugly stick? Alice looked like the whole tree fell on her! She was so ugly, she could make a railroad train turn down a dirt road! Her mother used to go everywhere with her, so she wouldn't have to kiss her goodbye!

HARE. (*After he and HATTER compose themselves*) But enough of this frivolity. We all know Alice, and we love her. She's a beautiful, beautiful person, and a dear, dear friend. We're happy to be able to honor this good friend—especially because of her great outlook on life—which can best be summed up in her now famous words, "Sometimes the light at the end of the tunnel can be from an oncoming locomotive!" (*Hare and Hatter applaud*)

HATTER. (*Gesturing to introduce Alice*) Alice... Ladies and gentlemen... (*While they applaud*) Is she beautiful..? Alice... (*To Alice*) Let's have lunch next week... (*They stop applauding and sit. ALICE has enjoyed their roast enormously*)

ALICE. You two are real funny. (*HARE and HATTER look at each other as if to say, "How do you like that?"*)

HARE. She thinks we're real funny.

HATTER. Sweetheart, funny is our business. It's our life. And we're pretty good at it, right?

ALICE. Yes, quite good.

HARE. Then maybe you can explain to us how come we've never been invited to perform at the castle, for the king and queen?

HATTER. Or how come we've never done a command performance? Or a lavish soiree? A gala benefit?

HARE. Never got a series.

HATTER. Or a movie.

HARE. Or the Merv Griffin Show.

ALICE. I don't know. But you're still real good.

(*Looking at the table*) Are you having a tea party?

HARE. Nah. It's from the deli. (*He crosses away from table*) You're welcome to a corned beef, help yourself ... (*Hare is getting thoughtful; ALICE considers a sandwich with not much enthusiasm*)

HATTER. (*To Alice*) See, we had this agent—he promised us the moon. We woulda settled for Cleveland. 'Couple of one nighters across the midwest, we could've had momentum. Blow into the Catskills—do heavy damage; next thing you know, everybody's talking about us. (*Imitating people talking about them*) "Did you catch the Hatter and the Hare? Man ya gotta see the Hatter and the Hare! Hysterical! Too much! Forget about it!!"

HARE. (*Coming back to add to the story*) But people don't understand, people don't know. I tell you, sister, there are a thousand comedians who don't have as much talent as we have in one finger! But they get the jobs; they get things. Because of jealousy. They're afraid of us. They're all afraid of us.

HATTER. Who's your favorite comedian?

ALICE. (*Thinks, then*) Popeye. (*Hare laughs a short, bitter, ironic laugh, and turns away*)

HATTER. (*Nodding*) You like Popeye, huh? (*She nods. To Hare*) She likes Popeye.

ALICE. (*To Hare*) Do you like Popeye?

HARE. (*Turns to her*) Do I like him? I think he's got the greatest material in the world. He should. He stole it from me.

ALICE. Popeye did?

HATTER. Stole his whole act. He (*Points to Hare*) was doing the pipe bit, (*Points to his own bicep*) the tatoo of the rowboat that turns into the battle ship—he did it in El Paso—(*Thinks*) The .. Top Hat Club.

HARE. (*Confirming*) Top Hat Club.

HATTER. (*To Alice*) Years before Popeye ever did it. *Years.*

ALICE. Gee . . . (*Shocked, then considers it*) But how could Popeye—

HARE. Forget it, forget it—makes me upset to think about it. It's over. (*Beat*) But they all stole from me, didn't they?

HATTER. All of them.

HARE. Jolson, Cantor, Milton Berle, Fred Flintstone . . .

ALICE. Fred Flintstone?

HATTER. And that other one . . .

ALICE. Barney Rubble?

HATTER. Jetson—George Jetson.

HARE. Oh, man, he was the worst.

HATTER. Meanwhile, where are *we* today?

ALICE. I'm glad you mentioned that. Where are we today? I mean—where are we?

HATTER. We're outside the castle.

ALICE. (*Turns and looks at the wall behind them. It's a section of a skyscraper—a granite-like facade*) It doesn't look like a castle . . .

HARE. That's just our nickname. What it really is is the corporate headquarters of the National Petroleum Group.

HATTER. (*Salutes the building mockingly*) Good old "NPG . . ." Where the king and queen decide what's right for all the rest of us.

HARE. (*Looking at the building*) Sometimes when I'm thinking what a crummy, dirty racket show business is, I think of this con game and I don't feel so bad. (*From the right, unbeknownst to Hare, Hatter and Alice; the royal entourage enters: KING, who's dressed like a king; QUEEN, dressed like a queen; P.R. MAN, wearing a business suit; and a STENO-GRAPHER with a steno pad. Also, the entire entourage are wearing gas masks. They stand listening to Hare and Hatter*)

HATTER. What a bunch of crooks.

HARE. Theives, snakes. Vermin.

HATTER. (*Turns to Alice*) And those are the opinions of their *friends*. (*And with that he notices the King and Queen, and tries to slide into another roast routine*) And friends, ladies and gentlemen, are what I think of whenever I see these two great humanitarians ... (*Moving toward entourage*)

QUEEN. (*Pointing at Hatter, talking through her gas mask*) Cut off his oil!

HATTER. (*Not quite understanding her*) Beg your pardon?

KING. (*Takes off his crown, pulls off mask, puts crown back on. To Queen*) Hey—we're outside. You can take that off now. (*QUEEN does. Then she points at Hatter again*)

QUEEN. Cut off his oil!

HATTER. I see that I really *must* beg your pardon ... (*Getting down on one knee*) Please—your pardon; your pardon!

QUEEN. My pardon my eye! (*She walks around to sit at table handing the gas mask to the P.R. MAN, who along with the STENOGRAPHER, has also taken his mask off*) These things are a nuisance. (*To P.R. Man*) You and your big ideas.

P.R. MAN. (*Following QUEEN; puts gas masks on table*) But it is a good idea. It was fully explained at the board meeting. Remember? People see the oil companies—including this oil company—as contributing to pollution. So, we pump smog into our own building, forcing all of us to wear gas masks, and that shows our commitment to the ideals of .. Of ... Of ...

KING. (*To P.R. Man, as he hands him his gas

mask) Will you be quiet? (*To Stenographer as he moves to sit by Queen*) How much money did we make today?

STENO. (*Looking at pad*) Hundreds of millions.

KING. (*Savoring it*) Hundreds of millions . . . Has a nice ring to it, wouldn't you say?

QUEEN. It's not enough. (*To King*) Fire somebody.

KING. I ought to fire you. You get the biggest salary here.

QUEEN. (*Looking at Alice*) Who are you?

ALICE. I'm Alice. Who are you?

QUEEN. Why, you impertinent little snip!

P.R. MAN. (*Stepping in, to Alice*) What the queen means is, the National Petroleum Group welcomes you to its corporate headquarters. (*Opens his brief-case*) Would you care for a copy of our annual report? (*Takes out a booklet, hands it to Alice*)

ALICE. (*Taking the booklet*) Thank you.

P.R. MAN. Thank *you*! Because at NPG, we believe an informed public is a public that's informed.

ALICE. (*Flipping pages*) But this book is empty. All the pages are blank.

QUEEN. (*Pointing to Alice*) Will somebody please cut off her oil!

KING. (*To Steno*) Make a note—the queen was fired at eleven-o-two; rehired at eleven-o-three.

STENO. (*Writing it down*) Fired . . . rehired . . . (*To King*) Anything else?

HARE. (*Jumping in as roastmaster again*) I'd just like to add one little thing—"You can always tell a comedian; but you can't tell him much!" (*HARE and HATTER laugh*)

HATTER. And you know, that reminds me—

QUEEN. (*To P.R. Man*) Would you please tell me why no one seems to understand how much it costs to drill for oil today?

P.R. MAN. (*Taking a file folder from his briefcase*) Certainly. This report explains the situation very clearly. (*Offers folder to Queen*)

QUEEN. (*Rejecting it*) So what's the reason?

P.R. MAN. We don't know.

KING. (*To Alice*) You aren't some kind of environmentalist, are you?

P.R. MAN. What the King means is, the National Petroleum Group makes every effort to consider the input of all concerned parties when deciding on company policies

ALICE. I don't know about that, but I would very much like to go home if someone could please show me the way.

HARE. (*Like Foster Brooks; staggering and singing*) "Show me the way to go home . . ."

HATTER. Say—I thought you didn't drink anymore.

HARE. Right. But I don't drink any less, either. (*They break up*)

QUEEN. How can they be so blind?

KING. Easy. They refuse to eat their carrots. (*To steno*) Make a note of that.

STENO. (*Dutifully taking it down*) Carrots . . .

QUEEN. There's only one way to handle this. (*Stands, points at Alice*) She must be made an example of!

KING. (*To Steno*) Make a note—the queen has spoken. Many times.

QUEEN. (*Pointing to Alice*) Seize her!

ALICE. Rubbish!

HARE. Caesar—Caesar. Now there was an emperor!

HATTER. And a terrific salad, too.

ALICE. You can't do a thing to me.

QUEEN. (*To King*) Are you going to let her talk that way to me?

KING. I'll handle this. (*Stands; to Alice*) Don't talk that way to her! Speak Spanish!

CHESHIRE CAT. (*Entering, Left, with pad at the ready*) Excuse me, but may I quote you on that, King?

KING. No! And it's "Mr. King" to you.

CHESHIRE CAT. Thank you! (*Writing on pad, moving Left*) This'll make a great article ... (*Envisioning headline*) "King Oil Reveals Entire Life Story ..." (*Exits, Left*)

P.R. MAN. (*To King*) Don't worry—I'll have public information issue an immediate denial. (*To steno*) Got that?

STENO. (*Writing*) Public information ... Immediate denial ... (*Looks up*) Will that be all?

P.R. MAN. Yes. Oh—and don't quote me. I'll deny it. (*He smiles*)

QUEEN. The matter has gotten quite out of hand.

KING. Quite out of hand.

HARE. (*A la Jack Benny*) Well ...

HATTER. That's a deep subject.

HARE. For such a shallow mind.

HATTER. On the other hand ...

HARE. Four fingers and a thumb.

HATTER. (*To Queen*) Are you *sure* you couldn't use a couple of top bananas like us at your next function?

QUEEN. (*Pointing at Hatter*) They get no gasoline for a year!

P.R. MAN. (*To Steno*) No gas for a year ...

STENO. (*Writing*) No gas for a year ...

ALICE. That's not fair.

QUEEN. (*Gloating at Hare and Hatter*) See how you like taking the bus!

HATTER. (*Resignedly*) That won't be necessary. (*To Hare*) Call me a taxi.

HARE. Alright, you're a taxi.

ALICE. They don't even need your old gasoline.

MOCK TURTLE. (*Entering, Right*) And when she

says "old gasoline," she means *old* gasoline.

P.R. MAN. (*Crossing to Turtle*) What the consumer advocate means is, occasionally it is the policy of this corporation to stockpile gas supplies.

KING. Have you all gone crazy? Doesn't anyone realize it's time for tennis? (*He takes a raquet from inside his robe, or under the table, and moves D.L.*)

MOCK TURTLE. Don't use that raquet—it could explode!

QUEEN. (*To Alice*) This is all your fault. You and people like you!

HATTER. People like her? People *love* her—she's beautiful—are you kidding? She's a beautiful, beautiful person.

CATERPILLAR. (*Entering, Right*) She is a beautiful person because she decided she is a beautiful person. She has raised her consciousness, and claimed her own space. (*To King*) And brother, with a grip like that, it's no wonder your backhand is off.

EAGLE. (*Entering, left, goes to Queen*) Your majesty, I have completed my time machine. (*Kneels*)

QUEEN. How far can you go in it?

DODO. (*Enters, left, singing*)
Five hundred miles;
Five hundred miles . . .

MOUSE. (*Entering, Left*) . . and so, my constituents, in re-entering the race for office, I say let's look at the record! And here it is . . . (*Takes out a record— 45 rpm—looks at it closely*)

QUEEN. (*Smugly, to Alice*) Maybe now you'll have some respect for the way things work around here.

DUKE. (*Entering with DUCHESS, moving threateningly toward Alice*) There she is!

DUCHESS. (*To Alice*) So what about it? How could you get me so upset? How??

DUKE AND DUCHESS. How? HOW??

WHITE RABBIT. (*Entering, looking up and around again*) Good news, bad news; good news, bad news. May I have your attention please—the good news is—they still haven't dropped the big one . . . The bad news is—(*Turns, looking off, R.*) We have a visitor from the East . . .

ARAB. (*Entering, in full Arabian desert garb, speaks with accent*) Greetings to all. I come to announce that we . . . (*Turns to Queen*) Are cutting off *your* oil.

QUEEN. You're pulling my leg . . .

ARAB. No. (*Takes an electrical plug from his robes*) We are pulling the plug. (*He disconnects the plug. Lights flicker. ARAB exits. Lights come down, then back up, then continue to flicker. General panic starts to build*)

QUEEN. I told you—I told all of you (*Points to Alice*)—It's her fault!

ALL. Her fault! It's her fault! (*The entire crowd starts moving toward ALICE. She backs toward exit*)

ALICE. Help! (*She rushes off. All follow. Lights go to black as announcer speaks*)

ANNOUNCER. (*Off Stage*) Was it Alice's fault? Will she get help? We'll find out after this . . . Intermission.

END OF ACT ONE

ACT TWO

In the darkness we hear the announcer's voice

ANNOUNCER. (*Off stage*) We return now to the Adventures of Alice, confident your intermission was pleasant, and somehow touched by General Products ... (*Stage lights up full to reveal bare stage with black and white chessboard background wall/flats. After a moment the RED QUEEN enters, jogging. She wears jogging togs, running shoes, and a crown. She jogs once around the stage then stops, U.C., and does some limbering-up, calisthentic type exercises. ALICE enters, left, running slowly and looking over her shoulder to see if she's being followed. RED QUEEN watches Alice a moment, then*)

RED QUEEN. Hate to tell you, dearie, but that's no way to jog.

ALICE. (*Turning*) I wasn't jogging—I was running.

RED QUEEN. Running, jogging. (*As if they're the same thing*) (*Crossing to Alice*) First of all you should get yourself a good pair of sweats. Like these. (*Indicating her own*)

ALICE. I don't think I'll be here that long.

RED QUEEN. That's what everybody says. Believe me, if you want to be a queen, you have to work at it. Take me for example. Perfect figure—twenty two inch waist. (*Confidentially*) You know what this waist was three years ago? Don't ask.

ALICE. Are you really a queen?

RED QUEEN. You got it.

ALICE. Well, it's nice to meet you. I'm Alice.

RED QUEEN. OK, Alice. So where do you want to start?

ALICE. Start what?

RED QUEEN. Your program.

ALICE. Program? Like a TV program?

RED QUEEN. (*Laughs*) No, dearie. Although, once you're a queen, anything can happen. Strangers open doors for you. Sales clerks are Johnny on the Spot. And your social life—well, we'll get into that later.

ALICE. You mean it really is possible to become a queen?

RED QUEEN. You're not listening, sweetie. You can become a queen anytime you want. I mean, down at my health club there are women who come in for their first visit looking like death warmed over. Six months, a year later—queens.

ALICE. That's hard to believe.

RED QUEEN. It just comes down to one thing: Me.

ALICE. You?

RED QUEEN. No, no—I mean, *you* have to say *"me."*

ALICE. Me?

RED QUEEN. Right. Except it's not "me, question mark." It's "me, exclamation point!" Me, me, me— you've gotta put yourself first. Ahead of everything.

ALICE. Everything?

RED QUEEN. You want to be a queen?

ALICE. Well . . .

RED QUEEN. You know what you are today if you're *not* a queen? You're a "them." One of the "others." A face in the crowd. I tell you, it's the only way.

ALICE. I guess it would be kind of fun.

RED QUEEN. Oh, it is. But more than that—it's something I do for me. It's a beautiful word, isn't it? (*Spells it*) M-e. Me!

ALICE. What does your husband think about . . . the idea?

RED QUEEN. Him?

ALICE. Uh-huh.

RED QUEEN. I don't know. Let him worry about him. I've got myself to think about. Except I will spare a few minutes to help you start thinking about you.

ALICE. There have been *so* many other things to think about here . . .

RED QUEEN. Exactly—now you've got to start to focus—all your thoughts, all your energies—on *you*.

ALICE. On me.

RED QUEEN. (*Moves D.C. with ALICE as she describes the plan of attack*) Right. Now, I'll make an appointment for you with Richard. He's the overall . . . body guy at the club—he can tell you what exercises you need, where you want to lose weight, where you want to bulk up. Then you'll sit with Monique—she's our health and beauty girl—lotions, creams, moisturizers—she's pretty good. Then, you'll talk to Donald. He's the nutritionist. You are what you eat, you know.

ALICE. No, I didn't know that.

RED QUEEN. In a matter of months, you can be a queen.

ALICE. Imagine . . .

RED QUEEN. (*Looking more closely at Alice*) Well, you are a little on the young side. Maybe a princess.

ALICE. I don't know what my friends would say if I were a princess . . not to mention a queen!

RED QUEEN. Not to mention your friends, but your friends have nothing to do with it. Friends are alright, but don't let them get in the way of your number one friend of all—you.

ALICE. What should I do first?

RED QUEEN. Doesn't make much difference. It's the basic idea that's important.

ALICE. OK.

RED QUEEN. And the basic idea is to start at square one ... (*She resumes some loosening-up exercises*)

ALICE. And go where?

RED QUEEN. Wherever you like. But—it can be farther than it looks ...

ALICE. Why?

RED QUEEN. Because you can't always count on the help of others ...

ALICE. But at least I have your help.

RED QUEEN. (*She focused on something other than herself for as long as she could; she's totally immersed in "me" again*) What's that .. ?

ALICE. I said at least have your help.

RED QUEEN. (*Doesn't recognize Alice now*) You're not collecting for some charity, are you? Because I didn't give at the office and I certainly don't plan to give here. (*She pats her hand under chin, as in a firming up effort*) Oh ... this chin!

ALICE. I meant about the club—becoming a queen.

RED QUEEN. Yeah, clubs .. sure. (*Starts jogging in place*) Sorry, but I have so many things to do ... (*Jogging off, Left*) For myself ... (*She exits*)

ALICE. (*Calling after Red Queen*) But I thought you said ... (*She turns center; thinking aloud*) A queen . . . I wonder if it really could happen . . . I wonder what people would call me ... (*Laughing*) I wonder what Dinah would think ...

GENTLEMAN DRESSED IN WHITE PAPER. (*Entering, Right; carries a clipboard and reads the answers to Alice's questions from it*) First question—yes; second question, "Queen Alice"; third question (*Looks up at Alice*) Who cares what a cat thinks, anyway?

ALICE. How did you do that?

GENTLEMAN. Do what?

ALICE. Answer my questions without hearing my questions.

GENTLEMAN. What makes you think I didn't hear the questions?

ALICE. You weren't here.

GENTLEMAN. (*Looking down where ALICE is about to step*) Don't step there! (*He bends down and picks something up. It's too small for us to see. He holds it out to Alice*) You almost stepped on a bug.

ALICE. (*Moving back*) I don't like bugs ...

GENTLEMAN. This kind won't hurt you. It's not a creepy-crawly bug, it's a listening bug.

ALICE. A listening bug?

GENTLEMAN. Electronic surveillance. That's how I heard your questions.

ALICE. (*Moving closer to look at it*) You could hear me through *that*?

GENTLEMAN. Not just this—there's hundreds of these things all over the place.

ALICE. Why?

GENTLEMAN. Because we want to know what you're talking about. (*Holding it for Alice to inspect*) These things are amazing. State of the art. This will pick up the sound of a cat walking across a foam rubber mat. Not only that—if a flea jumps off the cat, you can hear the flea hitting the mat. Now *that* is technology.

ALICE. Gee. But isn't it rude to listen in on other people's conversations?

GENTLEMAN. Yes. (*Consulting another page on clipboard*) At least, according to 68 per cent of the people we listened to who discussed the subject. Twelve percent had no strong feelings either way, and seventeen percent thought their entire lives were subject to scrutiny through one type of snooping or another.

(*Looks up; semi-confidential*) They pretty much have the correct view of the situation.

ALICE. But who wants to know all this? Who is it that's listening?

GENTLEMAN. Everybody.

ALICE. I'm not.

GENTLEMAN. I mean, there are business interests, political interests, military interests. Plus, a couple of old ladies in Pittsburgh who just like to listen.

ALICE. It seems kind of sneaky to me.

GENTLEMAN. You have no idea how sneaky. But somebody has to do it.

ALICE. Why?

GENTLEMAN. Because it's their job. And if they didn't do their job, somebody would see them—or hear them—not doing it. Right, Charlie?

ALICE. (*Looking around*) Who's Charlie?

GENTLEMAN. He's sitting in at my listening post right now while I'm talking to you. At least, he'd better be, or our supervisor will know the reason why.

ALICE. You mean even the listeners get listened to?

GENTLEMAN. More than anybody. We have access to so much information that they have to keep real close tabs on us. But I don't mind—hear that, Charlie? I don't mind—hear that, Mr. Brown? (*To Alice*) Mr. Brown is my supervisor, and a heckuva guy. I love my work.

ALICE. If you don't mind me saying so, I think it would be very dull.

GENTLEMAN. Sometimes. But there's always new conversations just around the corner. New secrets to hear, new news to record and pass along—new financial developments. You want to know how much somebody makes, you can look it up. You want to know who doesn't pay their bills, you can look it up. It's great.

ALICE. It is?

GENTLEMAN. Plus, I get a company car and everything. For example, consider the Red Queen you were just talking to. What kind of job security does a queen have? Oh sure, she goes out to good restaurants, she shops in the best stores. But twenty years down the road, she picks up a couple of pounds, wrinkles set in, the old face lift starts to droop. I have a terrific set-up. Seniority, steady money, and a good chance for promotion. I mean, what's your queen ever going to get promoted to?

ALICE. I'd still rather be a queen than a listener.

GENTLEMAN. You're entitled to your opinion. Just remember that a lot of other people will be listening to it.

ALICE. I don't care one bit if they do.

GENTLEMAN. (*Knowing smile*) You talk like one of my co-listeners—that is, one of my former co-listeners. Old Jim. Jim started saying he wasn't *real* happy with the shifts he had to work. Mr. Brown, my supervisor, had old Jim's every move monitored for two months. Every call, every visitor, every trip to the market. Somehow one thing led to another, and today old Jim's in jail. Locked up tighter than a drum.

ALICE. If your supervisor did that—

GENTLEMAN. He did.

ALICE. He must be a terrible man!

GENTLEMAN. Oh, no . . .

ALICE. Terrible and mean and nasty.

GENTLEMAN. Now, now . . .

ALICE. He must be some kind of monster!

GENTLEMAN. (*Forgetting the "listeners" for a mo-*

ment) Believe me, his *wife* is the monster! She *makes* the old coot act so crazy! Living with a woman like that could make anybody—(*Stops short. Realizes what he's saying—and who could be hearing it*) ..anybody see that Mr. and Mrs. Brown are the finest couple you'd ever want to meet!

ALICE. You don't mean it.

GENTLEMAN. I sure do. I said it, I meant it, and I hope they heard it. (*Livid at Alice, he shakes his fist at her as if he's gonna clobber her*)

ALICE. Why don't you tell the truth?

GENTLEMAN. That *is* the truth, little darling... (*Now makes a choking motion, like he'd like to wring her neck*)

ALICE. I don't care what you say, or do, or who you listen to! (*She folds her arms and moves to D.R.*)

GENTLEMAN. It's been nice talking to you ... (*Moves left, still gesturing menacingly*)

ALICE. It hasn't been very nice talking to you.

GENTLEMAN. Bye-bye ... (*Drops the pleasant tone of voice*) Charlie—put her down as a subversive! (*He exits left*)

ALICE. He can't hurt me one bit. (*Blackout, except for spot on ALICE, D.R.*) I wonder why it gets dark so quickly here..? (*TWEEDLEDUM and TWEED-LEDEE enter, Right, and begin rushing around in circles around ALICE*)

TWEEDLEDUM. Hurry!

TWEEDLEDEE. Hurry!

TWEEDLEDUM. Hurry!

TWEEDLEDEE. Hurry!

TWEEDLEDUM. Hurry!

TWEEDLEDEE. Hurry! (*Alice is getting dizzy watching them*)

ALICE. Please stop!

TWEEDLEDUM. (*They both look around*) Who said that?

TWEEDLEDEE. Who is it?

ALICE. Why . . . I said it.

TWEEDLEDUM. (*Puzzled, to Dee*) "I said it?"

TWEEDLEDEE. Normally a *mouth* would say it, and an *eye* would see it.

ALICE. No—I said it. Me. Alice.

TWEEDLEDUM. (*As they both size Alice up*) I don't know what to make of her.

TWEEDLEDEE. She looks healthy enough.

ALICE. You shouldn't make personal remarks.

TWEEDLEDUM. Do you own any fur coats?

ALICE. Of course I don't.

TWEEDLEDUM. (*Shaking his head*) I still don't know what to make of her.

ALICE. You could make me quite happy if you'd just leave me alone. Or—if you wouldn't mind—show me how to get to the Red Queen's health club.

TWEEDLEDEE. (*To Dum*) I've got it! (*To Alice*) How would you like to pass out literature—distribute pamphlets to passerbys?

ALICE. What kind of literature?

TWEEDLEDUM. Literature designed to save the whales.

TWEEDLEDEE. And the seals.

TWEEDLEDUM. And the dolphins, and the goldfish, and certainly the oysters.

TWEEDLEDEE. *Certainly* the oysters.

ALICE. Save them from what?

TWEEDLEDUM. From extinction!

TWEEDLEDEE. From destruction!

TWEEDLEDUM. From here to Eternity and back again!

ALICE. Well I wouldn't want them to be harmed.

TWEEDLEDEE. Harmed!

TWEEDLEDUM. (*To Dee*) This calls for an illustration. (*To Alice*) Please sit down . . . (*Alice sits as DUM and DEE move to D.C. in neat glides, with their arms around each others neck. Spot up D.C. as they sing—or recite*)

The sun was shining on the sea,
TWEEDLEDEE.

Shining with all his might:
TWEEDLEDUM.

He did his very best to make
TWEEDLEDEE.

The billows smooth and bright . . .
TWEEDLEDUM.

And this was odd,
TWEEDLEDEE.

Because it was
BOTH.

The middle of the night.
TWEEDLEDEE.

The Walrus and the Carpenter
Were walking close at hand;
They wept like anything to see
Such quantities of sand:
TWEEDLEDUM.

"If this were only cleared away,"
TWEEDLEDEE.

They said,
BOTH.

"It would be grand!"
TWEEDLEDUM.

"O, Oysters, come and walk with us!"
The walrus did beseech.
"A pleasant walk, a pleasant talk,
Along the briny beach."
TWEEDLEDEE.

We cannot do with more than four,

to give a hand to each."

The eldest oyster looked at him,
But never a word he said:
The eldest oyster winked his eye,
And shook his heavy head . . .
Meaning to say he did not choose
To leave the oyster bed.
TWEEDLEDUM.
But four young oysters hurried up,
All eager for the treat:
Their coats were brushed, their faces washed,
Their shoes were clean and neat . . .
And this was odd, because, you know,
They hadn't any feet.

Four other oysters followed them,
And yet another four;
And thick and fast they came at last,
And more, and more, and more . . .
All hopping through the frothy waves,
And scrambling to the shore.
TWEEDLEDEE.
The Walrus and the Carpenter
Walked on a mile or so,
And when they rested on a rock,
Conveniently low:
And all the little oysters stood
And waited in a row.

"The time has come," the Walrus said,
"To talk of many things;
Of shoes . . . and ships . . . and sealing-wax . . .
Of Cabbages . . . and kings . . .
TWEEDLEDUM.
And why the sea is boiling hot . . .

And whether pigs have wings.
TWEEDLEDEE.
A loaf of bread," the Walrus said,
Is what we chiefly need:
TWEEDLEDUM.
Pepper and vinegar besides
Are very good indeed . . .
BOTH.
Now if you're ready, Oysters dear,
We can begin to feed."
TWEEDLEDUM.
"But not on us!" the Oysters cried,
Turning a little blue.
"After such kindness, that would be
A dismal thing to do!"
TWEEDLEDEE.
"The night is fine," the Walrus said.
"Do you admire the view?"
TWEEDLEDUM.
"It seems a shame," the Walrus said,
"To play them such a trick,
After we've brought them out so far,
And made them trot so quick!"
TWEEDLEDEE.
The Carpenter said nothing but
"The butter's spread too thick!"

"I weep for you," the Walrus said,
"I deeply sympathize."
TWEEDLEDUM.
With sobs and tears he sorted out
Those of the largest size,
Holding his pocket-handkerchief
Before his streaming eyes.
BOTH.
"O, Oysters," said the Carpenter,

"You've had a pleasant run!
Shall we be trotting home again?"
TWEEDLEDEE.
But answer came there none ...
TWEEDLEDUM.
But answer came there none ...
BOTH.
And this was scarcely odd, because
They'd eaten every one.

*(They return, with neat glides, to D.R. and Alice.
She rises to greet them. During this, a swivel
chair containing the WHITE QUEEN is brought
onstage, U.C., in the darkened area. It remains
there, back to the audience)*

ALICE. I liked the Walrus best, because at least
he was a *little* sorry for the poor oysters.
TWEEDLEDUM. Then you'll help us?
TWEEDLEDEE. You'll hand out pamphlets?
TWEEDLEDUM. At the airport?
ALICE. I'm not sure about going to the airport.
You see—
TWEEDLEDEE. (*Interrupting*) Too late. (*To Dum*)
Lunchtime.
TWEEDLEDUM. Fish and chips?
TWEEDLEDEE. Perfect. (*They exit, left, in neat glides.
ALICE watches them go, speechless. After a moment
she turns center and a white shawl is thrown or
blown over her shoulder from offstage left. She picks
it up*)
ALICE. Why .. it's somebody's shawl ... I wonder
whose it is .. ?
WHITE QUEEN. (*Still U.C. with her chair turned
away*) My shawl will be returned by a girl named
Alice.

ALICE. (*Looking around for the source of that comment*) I'd be glad to return it if I ... knew where you were ...

WHITE QUEEN. (*Still in darkness*) It will be as if a lightbulb were suddenly turned on. (*Stage lights up full. ALICE sees chair, starts U.C.*) And she will find her way to me ... (*Alice gets to the chair and turns it around on its swivel. We see the Queen. She is dressed in white, with a white fright wig; her eyes are closed, and a bowling ball is on her lap*) ... This—all this I see ...

ALICE. Excuse me ...

WHITE QUEEN. (*Opening her eyes and seeing the shawl*) Hah! Worked again! (*Wanting the shawl*) I'll take that, thanks ... (*ALICE hands it to her*) I really can't thank you enough. I have to do something for you. Let's see .. what would you like to know about your future? That's my specialty.

ALICE. But, if I may—who are you?

WHITE QUEEN. I'm the White Queen. Also, a prophet of sorts. I can see the future. Unfortunately, I can't see the present, or I'd locate my crown.

ALICE. How do you do. (*Curtsies*) I'm Alice.

WHITE QUEEN. Oh, I know who you are. Saw it all right here in my crystal ball. (*Pats the bowling ball, looks down at it*) Darn! I did it again ...

ALICE. Did what?

WHITE QUEEN. Took the wrong ball this morning. This is a bowling ball. You know what that means?

ALICE. No.

WHITE QUEEN. In a few minutes, my husband will be going for a seven-ten split with my Cartier crystal ball.

ALICE. My goodness.

WHITE QUEEN. (*Closing her eyes; concentrating on the future, breathes a sigh of relief*) It's alright!

(*Opens her eyes*) He's gonna miss. (*To Alice*) Now, *you* would like to see your cat, Dinah. But you'd also like to be a queen. Wouldn't you?

ALICE. That's right.

WHITE QUEEN. Tell you what I'm gonna do. I'm gonna look into this—(*Stops, looks at bowling ball*) thing—and see what the future holds for you.

ALICE. Really?

QUEEN. (*Eyes closed; concentrating*) Silence ... I need silence ... (*Changer her mind. To Alice*) Actually, I need a comb. Do you have a comb or brush or anything? (*Closing her eyes*) Ah—wait—I already know the answer to that—you don't ... But I do! (*Opens her eyes and takes a brush from beside her on the chair*) Would you mind doing the honors? '(*Holding the brush out to Alice*)

ALICE. No, I love to brush hair. I brush Dinah every day.

WHITE QUEEN. (*Appalled, looks at brush*) Not with that brush, I hope.

ALICE. This is yours.

WHITE QUEEN. Right. Now, while you put my hair in order, I'll foretell the future.

ALICE. If I may, I'd especially like to know whether or not I'll ever be a queen. (*She starts on Queen's hair*)

WHITE QUEEN. (*Closing her eyes*) Let me give it some thought ... A lot of people don't realize what a precision game the prophecy business is. Did you know I predicted the first man on the moon?

ALICE. Really?

WHITE QUEEN. I have a list of successful predictions as long as your arm. (*Opens her eyes*) Wait a minute, let me see your arm. (*Looks at it*) Oh yeah—it's at least that long. (*Closes her eyes again*)

ALICE. (*Having trouble with the knots*) I'm not

having such good luck here, I'm afraid . . .

WHITE QUEEN. Don't worry, you will— I see you one day operating the finest hair salon in all of France.

ALICE. France??

WHITE QUEEN. OK, Rhode Island. (*Still concentrating*) You will have many children . . . you will name each of them Daphne . . and finally—you will find your way home from here.

ALICE. I will!?

WHITE QUEEN. Yes. But I can't tell you how.

ALICE. Oh, that's alright. Just to know I'll be able to see Dinah—

WHITE QUEEN. Just do me one favor.

ALICE. Of course.

WHITE QUEEN. Give me your honest opinion of my hair.

ALICE. Why . . .

WHITE QUEEN. Honest, now.

ALICE. Well, I think . . . your hair . . . is a fright.

WHITE QUEEN. I agree. (*Pulls the wig off. She wears a skull cap underneath—she looks totally bald*) If there's one thing I appreciate, it's candor. (*She stands, gestures for ALICE to sit*) Please, have a seat . . . (*ALICE does*) Now about you becoming a queen—it's really not much of a field.

ALICE. How about a princess then?

WHITE QUEEN. There's not much difference. Consider the Red Queen. Consider myself. If I were you, I'd stay right where you are. And keep your head. And your hair.

ALICE. (*A little disappointed*) Oh . . ?

WHITE QUEEN. Because you're a good egg. (*Closes her eyes*) And you're about to meet another good egg . . . (*QUEEN begins pulling the chair with Alice in it toward D.R. As she does, lights fade except for area D.R. From offstage Humpty Dumpty's wall is moved onstage, with HUMPTY sitting on top of it. Chair is turned so Alice doesn't see wall or Humpty)*

ALICE. But . . . Is this the way I should be going?

WHITE QUEEN. Trust me.

ALICE. . . alright.

WHITE QUEEN. And thanks for the styling. (*Stops. Feels her head*) My friends will be able to call me "Curly" again. (*Exiting, right*) Good luck . . .

ALICE. But . . . (*She turns in her chair and now sees Humpty on the wall*) Oh!

HUMPTY DUMPTY. (*Very seriously*) Oh . . ?

ALICE. You're Humpty Dumpty!

HUMPTY DUMPTY. Who wants to know?

ALICE.

"Humpty Dumpty sat on a wall;
Humpty Dumpty had a great fall."

HUMPTY DUMPTY. I had a terrible fall. A lousy winter. And a rotten spring.

ALICE. Why?

HUMPTY DUMPTY. Why do you think?

ALICE. Well according to the poem you had a great fall and all the king's horses and all the king's men couldn't put you back together again.

HUMPTY DUMPTY. That had nothing to do with it.

ALICE. Then what was it?

HUMPTY DUMPTY. You've got a nerve on you, you know that? You come traipsing up here, asking all these questions—

ALICE. Oh, I didn't traipse. I slid over in (*Turns to point to chair, but it's been pulled offstage with a string or wire*) . . in that chair . . . My, that's odd . .

HUMPTY DUMPTY. And we're even. State your business here; or beat it.

ALICE. Don't you think you'd be safer down on the ground? That wall looks kind of narrow.

HUMPTY DUMPTY. (*Picks up a sub machine gun with a strap and puts it over his shoulder*) Let somebody try and push me off this wall. Just let 'em try.

ALICE. (*Looking at gun*) Is that thing real? (*He doesn't answer. Instead, by way of response, he picks up a sawed-off shotgun and holds it across his chest, glaring at Alice*) Another one??

HUMPTY DUMPTY. Just like the Boy Scouts, I'm prepared.

ALICE. For a war, it looks like.

HUMPTY DUMPTY. You're catching on. (*Hearing something, he turns to U.L., points the shotgun and yells*) Freeze!!

ALICE. (*Looking that way*) What is it?

HUMPTY DUMPTY. (*Warily*) Maybe nothing . . . Maybe a sniper . . . (*Puts gun down, turns to Alice*) You were saying?

ALICE. If you're so afraid, why do you stay here?

HUMPTY DUMPTY. I'm not afraid!

ALICE. But those guns—and your nerves don't seem very calm.

HUMPTY DUMPTY. I'm ready, that's all. Ready and willing. This wall used to be full of eggs like me. They're gone now. Once this was a neighborhood you didn't have to be afraid to live in. That's over now. Except for me.

ALICE. Where did the other eggs go?

HUMPTY DUMPTY. Behind the wall. (*Looks down there*) They think it's safe there. Fools.

ALICE. Isn't it safe there?

HUMPTY DUMPTY. Of course not.

ALICE. Why?

HUMPTY DUMPTY. Because *they* can climb over the wall. They can drop molotov cocktails from on top of the wall. They can lob in a few mortars from a hundred feet away. That is, they could if it weren't for me. I'm not like your average egg. When I fall and break, a pair of panty hose isn't gonna pop out.

ALICE. You were talking about "they." Who is "they?"

HUMPTY DUMPTY. Good question. (*He looks around, a diligent sentry*)

ALICE. But you don't know the answer?

HUMPTY DUMPTY. In this day and age, you don't need to know *who* they are. You need to know *where* they are ... (*Thinks he sees something again*) Freeze!

ALICE. Why do you keep saying "freeze?"

HUMPTY DUMPTY. (*Looks at her with contempt*) Because I used to work in a popsicle factory. Don't you have anyplace else to go? It's not safe here.

ALICE. Where is it safe?

HUMPTY DUMPTY. Nowhere.

ALICE. Did you really work in a popsicle factory?

HUMPTY DUMPTY. Sure.

ALICE. What flavors did you make?

HUMPTY DUMPTY. Machine-gun mango.

ALICE. I never heard of that. I mean, I've heard of mango.

HUMPTY DUMPTY. Let me give you some advice.

ALICE. I've been getting a lot of that lately.

HUMPTY DUMPTY. Get yourself a good flak jacket.

ALICE. The Red Queen said I should get a good pair of sweats.

HUMPTY DUMPTY. Forget the Red Queen. Get a flak jacket, a nice light revolver, and a big dog.

ALICE. I already have a cat.

HUMPTY DUMPTY. Forget the cat. A big dog is what you want. A nice doberman. Then go home and lock your doors and windows.

ALICE. I'd love to go home, but I don't know how to get there.

HUMPTY DUMPTY. (*As if threatened*) Well *I* can't take you!

ALICE. (*Surprised*) That's alright...

HUMPTY DUMPTY. I'm not running some baby sitting service here!

ALICE. I didn't say you were.

HUMPTY DUMPTY. You're out walking around—no flak jacket, no gun—you don't even know the way home!

ALICE. Well I know I'm not welcome here! So good bye! (*She turns to walk U.C.*)

HUMPTY DUMPTY. Freeze!

ALICE. (*Turns*) You could frighten someone like that!

HUMPTY DUMPTY. (*Pulling in his horns; softer*) Don't you get it? That's the whole idea. If you scare *them*, they're not gonna realize how scared you are. And they'll leave you alone. And you won't become a victim.

ALICE. You shouldn't think about those things so much. Or maybe you *will* become a victim.

HUMPTY DUMPTY. (*Paranoia maxima*) Why? What'd you hear?? Who were you talking to!?

ALICE. No one! But look how edgy you are. That's no way to be.

HUMPTY DUMPTY. (*Looking around, a little sheepish*) I like you. I knew you were a good kid the first time I saw you. Here... (*Picks up a handgun and offers it to ALICE*) I want you to have this. Go on, take it.

ALICE. Oh, no. I couldn't.

HUMPTY DUMPTY. Go on! It could help you out. It could save your life. (*Smiling*) It's a lot of fun... (*Squeezes the trigger. It's a squirt gun*) Huh? See..?

ALICE. (*Laughing*) Well, thanks, but no thanks.

HUMPTY DUMPTY. You're sure now? (*She nods*) Well, in that case. (*Puts pistol into his belt, or down on the top of the wall*) It's time for me to get back to my eternal vigilance.

ALICE. You have to leave?

HUMPTY DUMPTY. 'Gotta cover all your flanks, kid. (*His wall is moving slowly offstage, right*) See ya around . . . (*Shakes his head a little sadly*) I tell ya, it's lonely at the top . . .

ALICE. (*Waves*) Goodbye . . . (*HUMPTY is off. ALICE looks around*) Oh, I wish I knew which way to go . . .

WHITE KNIGHT. (*Entering, right, pulling a soap box derby kind of car with square wheels*) I'd be happy to take you the way I'm going.

ALICE. Which way is that?

WHITE KNIGHT. I really have no idea at this point . . . (*As he pulls the car, by a rope, toward U.C., full stage lights come up and Alice walks with him*)

ALICE. But if you don't know where you're going—

WHITE KNIGHT. I didn't say that. I know exactly where I'm going. I just don't know exactly how I'll get there.

ALICE. Well, I was just talking to Humpty Dumpty—

WHITE KNIGHT. (*Trying to place the name*) Humpty Dumpty . . ? Humpty Dumpty . . .

ALICE. Sat on a wall? Had a great fall?

WHITE KNIGHT. No. I'm not familiar with the case. Although, if this Humpty person was injured in an on-the-job environment, our agency wouldn't handle the case anyway.

ALICE. (*They are stopped now U.C.*) Agency?

WHITE KNIGHT. I'm with the government office of feasibility studies and probability reports. The agency for this Dumpty person would be the Occupational Safety and Health Administration.

ALICE. Oh.

WHITE KNIGHT. (*Proudly*) You've probably heard about our agency.

ALICE. I'm not sure.

WHITE KNIGHT. You're not? (*Gestures for ALICE to have a seat in the car*) Please sit down, I'll tell you all about it.

ALICE. In this?

WHITE KNIGHT. Of course. (*Proudly*) This is our latest project—we call it "Feasibility One." (*Indeed, the name is written on the side*) But more on that later.

ALICE. (*Getting into it*) This looks pretty neat . . .

WHITE KNIGHT. Why, our office comes up with some of the neatest stuff—I mean—some of the most noteworthy data—you've ever heard of. For example, we recently put more than ten thousand man hours into a report on why monkeys sleep with their eyes closed.

ALICE. (*She's more interested in the car than in his story*) . . Really . . .

WHITE KNIGHT. It's in the Congressional Record.

ALICE. Does this thing really run?

WHITE KNIGHT. We'll get to that in a minute. We conducted an exhaustive investigation into the cause of Eskimos contracting chapped lips.

ALICE. (*Trying to honk the steering wheel*) It doesn't have a horn, does it?

WHITE KNIGHT. No. And, we were responsible for the government investing three years of research to come up with the definitive study on what makes some mosquitos try to bite department store mannikins.

ALICE. Mosquitos . . .

WHITE KNIGHT. Exactly. So I'm sure you understand now that when you spoke of that Humpty person earlier, you could not have been thinking of the government office of feasibility studies.

ALICE. Could I drive this?

WHITE KNIGHT. Ah—now we come to this. Feasibility One. She's a beauty, isn't she.

ALICE. How fast will it go?

WHITE KNIGHT. Oh, speed is not the purpose of this vehicle. In fact, just the opposite.

ALICE. You mean it's supposed to go slow?

WHITE KNIGHT. Strictly speaking, it's not supposed to go at all.

ALICE. It's not?

WHITE KNIGHT. Have you noticed the wheels?

ALICE. (*She looks*) Square wheels?

WHITE KNIGHT. (*Proudly*) Square wheels.

ALICE. Why?

WHITE KNIGHT. Let's say you're a family man. It's Sunday, and you decide to take your family out for a ride. Wouldn't you think twice if that were your car?

ALICE. I'm sure I would.

WHITE KNIGHT. And why?

ALICE. Because not even a family of midgets could fit in this car.

WHITE KNIGHT. No, no—that's not it. The point is— the car has square wheels. How could any car with square wheels go rolling merrily along?

ALICE. It couldn't.

WHITE KNIGHT. Precisely. A car like that would be very difficult to move.

ALICE. I can see that.

WHITE KNIGHT. So, the more people we can get to put square wheels on their cars, the more people who won't be taking their cars out so much, and the more fuel that won't be consumed. It's a brilliant idea— brought to you by your government office of feasibility studies. (*Real proud now*)

ALICE. And it was your idea?

WHITE KNIGHT. Oh, not just mine! Why, hur of the best minds in government toiled long hours to come up with this concept.

ALICE. (*Getting out of the car*) Well, regardless of whose idea it was, I'm afraid it's the craziest thing I ever heard of.

WHITE KNIGHT. Crazy?!

ALICE. (*She rubs her temples; it's all starting to get to her*) I'm afraid all this is beginning to get to me...

WHITE KNIGHT. It's nothing short of brilliant, is what it is... (*Takes the "tow" rope and begins pulling car off, left*)

ALICE. (*Seeing KNIGHT leaving*) I'm sorry. But my head hurts...

WHITE KNIGHT. We'll save tons and tons of energy, you wait and see!

ALICE. (*Rubbing her stomach*) And my stomach...

WHITE KNIGHT. And it wouldn't surprise me a bit if I got a promotion out of it! (*He exits*)

ALICE. (*Looking around*) I think I should lie down...

PITCHWOMAN. (*Enters, right. Carries a hand microphone and is a standard TV commercial person*) Hi, I'm Elizabeth Pleasant, and I'd like the chance to prove to you that (*Next to Alice now*) for your headache and upset stomach, you don't need to lie down—you need new, super-strength, fast-acting, "Aspirin And Then Some." (*To off right*) Ladies—if you would? (*TWO WOMEN enter wheeling a cart with three cardboard boxes on it. One is marked "brand x," one "brand y," and one "Aspirin and Then Some." They wheel car to D.C. They look like the commercial girls on "Price is Right," or any game show where products are given away. Pitchwoman continues to Alice*) Yes, new "Aspirin and Then Some" contains "Wonderol," which has special ingredients to help you fight back against those pesky head and stomach symptoms. (*To women*) Right, ladies?

BOTH. (*Smiling pleasantly*) We're being held captive against our wishes.

PITCHWOMAN. (*Moves to cart*) As you can see, here are boxes marked brand x, brand y, and "Aspirin and Then Some." Brand x is in a white box. Brand y too. But look at the pretty blue box "Aspirin and Then Some" is in. Isn't it, ladies?

BOTH. (*Still smiling*) We'd like to escape the first chance we get.

PITCHWOMAN. Exactly. (*To Alice*) So for that run-down feeling, which would you choose—potatoes, or stuffing?

ALICE. Ah . . .

PITCHWOMAN. Why—"Aspirin and Then Some!" Take it from us . . . (*She picks up the "Aspirin and Then Some" box. There's nothing under the box. She takes a bite out of the box, then spits out the piece of cardboard*) "Aspirin and Then Some," right, ladies?

BOTH. (*Still smiling*) Watch out, a piano is falling on you.

PITCHWOMAN. Of course it is. (*To Alice*) Remember —"Aspirin and Then Some."

ALICE. (*Backing away, left*) I think that I . . . I . . .

PITCHMAN. (*Entering, left, taking ALICE by the arm and finishing her sentence*)—would like a much brighter, whiter wash to get rid of that headache and upset stomach—(*Serious*) and that persistent itch or occasional discomfort. (*Smiling as if into a camera*) Hi, I'm Bob Armstrong (*He has led ALICE to the cart again, where he picks up two hand towels from cart*), and if you'll just hold onto these towels, I'll show you how a whiter wash is possible.

ALICE. I don't need a whiter wash.

PITCHMAN. Well, well! With four children, you must know what heavy stains are about!

ALICE. I must?

PITCHMAN. (*Puts one towel down*) Watch. (*Holds other towel out to ALICE*) See this towel? (*Puts it behind his back*) Well now you don't! (*Puts it down, picks up other towel*) But—this towel was washed in new Blixo! How's that headache feeling *now*?

ALICE. Ah . . .

PITCHMAN. You know, you've been such a good sport about all this, would you let us send you a case of new Blixo—to your home—and you'll pay us double the regular price? (*PITCHMAN and TWO LADIES applaud*)

ALICE. . . . I don't understand . . . (*PITCHMAN and PITCHWOMAN back off, still applauding, toward right exit. LADIES wheel cart off. ALICE stands watching them, bewildered. From the left, THE RED QUEEN enters. She is in a chair, being carried by the GENTLEMAN IN WHITE PAPER, THE WHITE KNIGHT, and TWEEDLEDUM and TWEEDLEDEE*)

RED QUEEN. (*To Alice*) On the other hand, sweetie, if you really want to lose the "blahs," you've got to get yourself some lackies to carry you around. (*PITCHMAN and GROUP are off, right. Others have put down Queen's chair in the same spot Alice's living room chair was in at home. It should be the same chair, with only a throw or sheet covering it. To Alice*) What do you think?

ALICE. I think I'd like to become a queen as soon as possible, so I can get home as soon as possible.

RED QUEEN. Ah—not so fast . . . (*She gets out of chair and gestures for ALICE to sit in it*) Please . . . (*ALICE sits*) Now of course you'd like to become a queen. But the question is—what have you done for *you* lately?

GENTLEMAN DRESSED IN WHITE PAPER. (*Stepping up with his clipboard*) I can tell you that. Where would you like to begin? What would you like to know?

TWEEDLEDUM. She volunteered to help us at the airport.

TWEEDLEDEE. (*To Gentleman in White Paper*) What's her position on saving the whales?

WHITE KNIGHT. I *know* she's not much on saving energy. (*His feelings are still hurt*)

WHITE QUEEN. (*Entering, left; fright wig is back on. She is walking with her eyes closed, concentrating*) I see ... I see ... (*She bumps into Alice's chair*)

RED QUEEN. You see as well as a bat!

WHITE QUEEN. (*Indignant, concentrates again*) I see ... that they will divorce ... there will be a scandal ... one of them will re-marry ... he will be elected ... there will be an earthquake ... a mining disaster ... and a flood ... (*Opens her eyes*) Then again, maybe not.

TWEEDLEDEE. How do you like them apples?

TWEEDLEDUM. Never mind apples—(*To White Queen*) what's the price of shrimp gonna do?

WHITE KNIGHT. I once directed a study at the agency concerning the effect of saltwater on Siamese shrimp.

GENTLEMAN DRESSED IN WHITE PAPER. I hope you're getting all this down, Charlie.

RED QUEEN. (*To Alice*) *Now* do you feel qualified?

ALICE. (*Stifling a yawn*) I feel sleepy ...

WHITE QUEEN. (*To the others*) She feels sleepy!

ALL. She feels sleepy!!

RED QUEEN. A hand for Alice! (*They applaud once, in unison*)

WHITE QUEEN. A wig for Alice! (*She tosses her wig into Alice's lap*)

TWEEDLEDUM AND TWEEDLEDEE. Three cheers for Alice!

ALL.   Hip-hip, hooray! Hip-hip, hooray! Hip-hip- (*Blackout. All exit but ALICE. Her living room is re-set in the spot D.L. The fright wig is struck, Dinah, a cat, replaces it on Alice's lap. During this, we hear ANNOUNCER'S VOICE*)

ANNOUNCER. (*Off stage. Immediately after black-out*) We interrupt this program, and we don't have to tell you why. Except to say

"Beware the jabberwock, my son
The jaws that bite, the claws that catch.
Beware the jubjub bird and shun
The frumious Bandersnatch."

This is our guarantee. Because we believe in motherhood, apple pie (*Lights start up on Alice living room set. ALICE asleep with Dinah on her lap*), and new, improved Acme cat food...the one cat food (*ALICE awakens, sees where she is, jumps up and turns off TV, cutting off announcer mid-sentence*) that no kitty can resist—remember—that's new—

ALICE. (*Delighted, hugging cat*) It was a dream! A dream .. !

ANNOUNCER. (*Off stage*) Sure it was . . . (*ALICE looks around uncertain, then shrugs, and hugs cat as lights fade*)

CURTAIN

www.ingramcontent.com/pod-product-compliance
Lightning Source LLC
Chambersburg PA
CBHW072152130726
47909CB00004BB/1623